To Jack & Jimmy

Timothy Young

The ANGRY Little PUFFIN

Written & Illustrated by

Timothy Young

Dedicated to my friends, all of them, but especially to
Frank Hernandez and Sam Aaron, two of my best and oldest friends.

Library of Congress Control Number: 2014941533

Designed & Illustrated by Timothy Young
Type set in GoodDog/Pigpen

ISBN: 978-0-7643-4805-1
Printed in China

Published by Schiffer Publishing, Ltd.
4880 Lower Valley Road
Atglen, PA 19310
Phone: (610) 593-1777; Fax: (610) 593-2002
E-mail: Info@schifferbooks.com

What's that–
some kind of penguin?
Oh, it's a sweet
little penguin!

Hey, what a kooky little penguin!
That's a funny-looking penguin!

If one more person calls me a penguin...I don't know what I'll do.

Look at the cute, little penguin!

THAT'S IT!
I CAN'T TAKE
IT ANYMORE!

All day long I hear
"Look at the funny
little penguin!"
and "What a
silly-looking
penguin!"

I AM
A PE

NOT

NGUIN!

I AM A PUFFIN!

P-U-double F-I-N!

Puffins are definitely not penguins.

It's bad enough I have to live in the PENGUIN HOUSE at the zoo and watch their lame-brained antics.

People don't even read the sign on my window! They just assume I'm a penguin.

I mean, there are so
many differences!

For one thing, penguins live
in the Antarctic,
near the very
bottom of the Earth.

Puffins live
on the top of
the world!

We're
polar
opposites!

It makes me so mad that
I could jump off a cliff,
but do you know what
would happen if I did?

I'D FLY AWAY!

That's right, puffins can fly!
Not like those dopey penguins
who seem to have forgotten how!

Why bother being a bird
if you can't even fly?

I don't know why penguins get all the attention...toys, movies, television...even comic books. It's penguins, penguins, penguins!

C'mon, THE PUFFIN would be the coolest guy in any comic book!

IT'S NOT FAIR!

For once, I'd like someone to come up and say, "Look! It's a puffin!"

Look, Daddy! It's a PUFFIN!

Puffins are my favorite! They're really neat and they live in the Arctic Ocean.
This one is an Atlantic puffin. He's also called a Common puffin.

I think he should be called a Special puffin. Look how cute he is!
There are other kinds too, like the Tufted puffin and the Horned puffin, but I like this one best!
He eats fish and squid and sand eels and he makes his home in cliffs near the ocean, and you know what, Daddy? He can fly, unlike those penguins over there.

He's so sweet! I wish I could have a pet puffin!

WOW, YOU SURE KNOW A LOT ABOUT PUFFINS!

LET'S GO SEE IF THEY HAVE A TOY PUFFIN IN THE GIFT STORE.

Hey, what's that?

It's some kind of penguin, I guess.

Well, he sure is a happy little penguin!